Terror at

White Otter Castle

Bonnie Ferrante

ISBN 978-0-992103 7-1-2

Revised

Other Books by Bonnie Ferrante

Nightfall - Dawn's End Book 1
Poisoned - Dawn's End Book 2
Outworld Apocalypse - Dawn's End Book 3
Bouquet (short story collection)
Inhale (short story collection)

Dedication

For my brother, John, whose courage, fortitude, and positive attitude are inspirational.

Chapter One

As the canoes threaded through the yellowing lily pads and marsh grass, an uneasy silence fell upon the paddlers. Ahead loomed White Otter Castle, the mysterious hundred-year-old monstrosity hidden away in isolated northern Ontario wilderness. The presence of the long-departed James Alexander McOuat pressed down upon the group as they neared the disintegrating structure. Grey logs with missing chinking, vanished shingles, gaping empty windows, and a partially collapsed awning spoke of decay, loss, and neglect.

It was late on the third afternoon of their canoe trip when the group reached the forlorn castle of broken dreams. Laurel, Aster, and Beth were suitably impressed. It was more imposing than its pictures, a massive log building remote by even northern standards. Built by hand by a single man in 1914, there were still no roads leading to its isolated site. It could only be reached by float plane, boat, canoe, helicopter, four—wheeled drive, or, in winter, by snowmobile. The otherworldliness of the log castle emphasized that they were far, far away from civilization as they knew it.

All the canoes stopped as the occupants gazed on this bizarre structure in the middle of nowhere. The plop plop of the paddles ceased. A light breeze swayed the leaves on the deciduous trees on shore and created small waves on the clear empty lake. Overhead, a turkey vulture circled silently.

Three red roofs contrasted vividly with the green foliage of trembling aspen, white birch, white ash, cedar, and spruce trees. A long red-roofed open porch/awning sheltered three dark doorways into the decrepit main building, which was also red-roofed. But what was most startling was the four-storey square tower in the back corner, facing the lake, seemingly transposed from the secluded Scottish highlands. One could imagine an imprisoned princess gazing out over the lake and woods or a mad poet pacing in frustration.

"Hold the canoe still," cried Aster. She took off her sunglasses and set them on top of her large straw hat. "I want to get some photos from the lake."

Matt, the handsome, blond stranger Aster had been partnered with, steadied the canoe by laying his paddle flat on the surface of the water. Aster pulled out her camera and shot several angles. Then she turned the camera on Matt and snapped two more. Her black wavy hair contrasted beautifully with her smooth, pale skin. Her face belonged in a Renoir painting.

"Oh, brother," said Beth as she resumed and paddled past with Laurel in the stern. "It's not enough she's got a gorgeous boyfriend at home, she has to hit on her canoe partner too."

"Sh," said Laurel. "She's just taking pictures. That's what she does."

"Right," said Beth. "She's going to add shots of hot Matt to her portfolio."

"Why not?" snapped Laurel. "He is photogenic."

"Uh huh."

The guides, Rebekkah and Steve, resumed paddling first. They led the canoes toward the landing through floating arrowhead. Laurel was first to break the silence. "Jimmy McOuat didn't build the red roofs." She tucked a strand of bright auburn hair behind her ear. "They were put on by the Ministry of Natural Resources in the 1950s to stop the castle from decaying away. Although it looks in pretty rough shape, there have been attempts to stop it from falling apart."

Beth, a wide-shouldered strong woman with short, wiry brown hair, nodded absently. She rubbed the back of her neck, trying to smooth out the small hairs that had risen at the sight of the weird castle.

Even without the red roofs, the castle would have been a marvel for its time. What would possess a man to build a monstrosity so far away from any community with only himself to rattle around in its large, lonely rooms? And what was the purpose of the odd tower?

Beth shivered as a small silhouette with a floppy hat appeared in the top tower window and just as quickly disappeared. The guides had said tourist season was pretty much over. The long weekend at the beginning of September was their slowest time. She could see no campsite on the shore, and no canoe pulled up on the bank. The shadow must have been a trick of the light.

"All right," called Aster as she resumed paddling. "Let's bring her in and check this colossal out. I can't wait to get some shots up close. This is phenomenal."

Beth rolled her eyes. This was only the middle of the third day of their trip and she was already longing to go home. She'd had enough of chirpy little Aster.

No one spoke as the three canoes touched the bank. The canoeists in the bows jumped onto the shore, pulled the canoes up onto the pebbly beach, and held the vessels while the paddlers in the stern made their way carefully along the keel and onto land. Together they hauled the craft further up the beach.

* * * * *

Laurel was tired of playing referee. It had been Laurel's idea to go on a five day wilderness canoe trip before the three friends went their separate ways after graduating. She, Aster, and Beth had been best friends since grade one when they formed "The Power Triangle", their protection against bullies or cliques. The idea had come to them when their teacher explained that triangles were the strongest shapes. Whenever one shouted out the cry, "Triangle Power", the other two were honour bound to come to her rescue, whatever the situation. Other students soon learned that to take on one of the girls really meant taking on all three. Laurel was the negotiator. Aster could verbally strip bark off a tree. And Beth was the enforcer. So how had things gone so wrong?

This last year of high school had been darkened by squabbles and resentment. Beth was barely speaking to Aster and Aster seemed bewildered and sad. Laurel, stuck in the middle, feared that once they went their separate ways, a thirteen year friendship would disintegrate. In a desperate hope to mend things, she convinced the other two to join her on a five day canoe trip to the wilderness.

So far the trip had been pretty cool and everyone had been looking forward to White Otter Castle. Beth and Aster didn't speak as they paddled and portaged, but being in separate canoes would have made it difficult anyway. Perhaps Laurel should have gone with Matt and forced the others together. Without teamwork, it was pretty impossible to get anywhere in a canoe.

As Laurel untied and carried her packsack and sleeping bag up onto the open space in front of the castle, she glanced toward the century-old structure. The empty black windows seemed to stare back at her. Maybe she should have read less about its creator's difficult life and sad, lonely death.

After a dinner of tuna, bannock, and carrots prepared by the guides, Rebekkah and Steve, everyone helped set up camp. Beth, Aster, and Laurel had one tent. Rebekkah and Steve shared one. Maxine, a woman in her mid-thirties, and her older husband Ted, shared another. Matt, Maxine's younger brother, had his own pup-tent.

"Make sure all your food, soap, and anything that might attract bears is in your packsacks," said Steve, as he had the last two nights.

"I know," said Laurel. "Tie it high in a tree away from the tents."

She tried not to notice Matt helping Aster with hers. The girl couldn't help being short after all.

Laurel used cocoa butter cream on her sore hands before tucking it into the sack. Paddling was giving her blisters on her palms in addition to sore shoulders. She spent too much time with books and not enough time challenging her body.

She watched Beth toss the rope over the limb with the first shot and pull the heavy pack up without any strain. The muscles in her bare arms flexed. Beth did most of the work paddling, but she hadn't complained. It might have been a different story if Beth had been matched with Aster.

Three days of paddling and portaging had taken its toll. It was time to chillax. Laurel read her e-book while Aster continued to photograph the structure and surroundings as the evening light changed.

"Don't go inside," warned Steve. "Boards could come down on you at any second. The stairs have rotted and most of the floors are gone. One wrong step and we'll have to telephone for a Medivac. That doesn't look good on our website."

"Alrighty," called Aster as she flopped down on her stomach, rolled over, and shot several angles of the tower.

Beth, a competitive swimmer and diver who would be attending Boston University next week on an athletic scholarship, swam in the cool lake as the setting sun turned the water into liquid gold. She was unaware that several of Aster's photographs caught her silhouetted against the gleaming lake. Laurel watched Aster pause, as though admiring Beth's smooth strokes through the water. Was Aster oblivious to how much Beth's feelings had changed toward her? Or did she even care? Out here, cut off from the rest of the world, under the shadow of that creepy castle, was not the place to cut loose your friends.

Chapter Two

Aster knew something was wrong but she thought it best not to poke at things with a stick. That's how you got stung. Beth had always been moody and Aster knew her home environment was less than ideal. If she wanted to talk, she would. Otherwise it seemed best to just try to cheer her up and get her to appreciate this trip.

A five day canoe trip had seemed pretty daunting. Aster was no more athletic than Laurel. Beth was their champion. Laurel reasoned with people, Aster verbally cut them to size, and if that didn't work, Beth had been the one who truly intimidated the bullies into backing down.

She watched Beth slice through the water, powerful, sleek, and beautiful. What did it feel like to have a body like that?

The girls were pretty decent baseball players. Laurel could hit and catch while Aster was the team's best pitcher. Beth focussed most of her attention on swimming and diving, but was a great runner when she hit the ball. But, Aster knew that if her friend had chosen to focus on baseball, she would have left Aster in the dust. Baseball had been just for fun. Water sports had been Beth's compulsion.

At her parent's insistence, Aster had been a Girl Scout, starting as a Spark at age five and completing the Ranger program last year. She might not be a great woodchopper, but she could start a fire with one match, pitch a tent in the rain, and tie a dozen different kinds of knots. Her passion, though, had always been photography. Aster lifted her camera, concentrating on line, focus, light, and framing. This place, this castle, called to her like a dark siren.

Aster had already shot fifty or sixty pictures since sighting the castle. It had an aura of history, power, mystery, and loss. She crept closer to the collapsing awning, focussing in on the darkened doorways.

"Not too close," called Steve.

She waved absently. Why did everyone think she was so helpless? Just because she was small and pale, wispy really, didn't mean she couldn't take care of herself. That's one of the reasons she had stuck with Girl Guides, deliberately choosing the most challenging badges to earn. But still, everyone assumed she needed help with the simplest tasks.

She wished she was going away to university like her friends. Laurel was going all the way across the country to Vancouver to study drama. Beth was going to another country for cripes sake. But she, dull little Aster, would be living in the same bedroom she'd been in for the last eighteen years, travelling the same roads, and eating at the same restaurants, all without her best friends. Sure she was glad to have been accepted in the media program at the college. It was one of the best in the country and many graduates had done very well for themselves. But, she couldn't help feeling left behind.

Everyone did their own thing as dusk approached. Then Rebekkah and Steve set up and ignited a campfire.

"Gather around, everyone," called Rebekkah.

Maxine and Ted approached hand-in-hand. Aster felt a twinge of envy as she followed the couple. She wondered how long they'd been together.

"Come on, Matt," Maxine called to her brother who was now stretched out on the grass, his hat over his face.

"Yes, bossy." He sat up with a grin.

Aster smiled. Even though he hassled his older sister, everyone could tell they were close. Beth and Laurel quickly joined the circle as the canoeists sat on the grass.

As usual, the guides told them about tomorrow's paddle. Then Laurel read trivia she had amassed about their surroundings. Aster had been awed at the Aboriginal rock paintings they'd seen on the way, knowing a people long, long forgotten had left their hunting images for generations to see. White Otter Castle was a different experience. Jimmy McOuat had built it by hand with logs from the surrounding woods. He pulled them from the dense forest with a homemade hand-winch and prepared the lumber for the roof, stairs, and floor with a whipsaw. Just as impressive, the twenty-six windows had been carried over fifteen portages from the closest town of Ignace.

"Why?" asked Matt, as he ran his hand through his blond curls. "Why so extravagant?"

"Some people say he wanted to prove a prediction wrong that he would die in a shack," said Laurel. "Others believe he was building it for a woman in Scotland, though that doesn't make sense to me since he tried to get a mail order bride. He wanted to marry a woman named Jane, but when he declined meeting her family, she married someone else."

"Yikes," said Aster. "What woman would want to live all the way out here?" She took out a wet wipe from her pocket and scrubbed her milky complexion, removing the heavy-duty sunscreen. Laurel passed her a can of insect repellent. Aster stepped back from the group and sprayed every bare spot of flesh. The nasty vermin seemed to have a special liking for ultra-white skin.

"It's a pretty great house for its time," said Beth.

"Truly impressive," said Ted. His salt and pepper hair was receding but his body showed a man who worked out. "I do a little carpentry and this blows me away. The logs at the corners are dovetailed, for heaven's sake, and I can't guess how much they weigh."

Laurel ran her flashlight over her booklet and announced, "Sixteen hundred pounds to a ton."

Ted snorted. "Unbelievable. That's a man with determination."

"And a whole lot of crazy," said his wife, Maxine.

"Maybe that's why people think it's haunted," said Laurel.

Everyone groaned.

"Really," said Laurel. "I read about sightings of Jimmy's ghost on the internet. He was a short, quiet man. This is what he looked like." She shone the flashlight on a black and white photograph as she held the booklet up for all to see. A slim man with a high forehead, thinning hair, a bushy moustache, and a pointy chin looked back.

Aster felt a sense of pride that a man of small stature could have completed such a daunting task on his own.

"He looks like a gentle man," said Maxine.

"He was," said Laurel. "It says: Intelligent, soft-spoken, and welcoming."

"Well, I hope he welcomes us then," said Matt, "because I'm heading to bed and I don't want anyone rattling chains in the night."

Laurel chuckled. "It's a full moon, too."

Aster frowned. Since night had fallen, the forest seemed to close in on them. She glanced at Matt. She didn't envy him sleeping alone in a tent. She was glad she would be beside her BFFs. If something came for her out of the darkness, she wanted Beth and Laurel within arm's length.

Steve lit the kerosene lamp so that everyone could find their way to their tents for the night. He and Rebekkah doused the campfire with buckets of water.

Inside the little tent, Aster flicked on her flashlight.

"Put that off," snapped Beth. "I really don't want to do a shadow strip show for everyone in the camp."

"Sorry," said Aster as she clicked it off.

At least Beth and Laurel had something worth looking at. Aster's mother had called her a late bloomer when she was the last girl in the class to get a training bra.

"Don't worry," she had said. "You'll catch up in time."

Aster slipped her bra out from under her T-shirt and smoothed it down. She never really had caught up. Even though Beth was muscular and trim, she had better boobs than Aster. And Laurel. Aster sighed. The only description for her was sizzling hot. Red-haired, curvy, with a wide smile that could light up a city.

Aster climbed into her cold sleeping bag and pulled it up to her chin. They slept with their feet toward the entrance so that no one would have to climb over anyone else if they had to go during the night. Aster shivered at the thought. She avoided drinking anything after supper so she would never have to face the woods at night and bare her bottom to bugs and snakes. She never told the other two how afraid she was of the forest after dusk. They thought she had outgrown it, but there was something about the fact that creatures of the night were hidden and watching when you were at your most vulnerable. She had hated when the other Girl Guides told spooky stories in the dark.

The first two nights of camping had been okay but this place gave her the creeps. She hated the thought of all those empty black windows in the castle staring down at her. Beth snorted in her sleep and Laurel's breathed heavily. She realized she was the only one still awake.

Rocking trees creaked in the wind, water slapped against the beach, and the forlorn cry of a loon echoed over the lake. Aster tossed and turned, cursing the tree root under her hip. Steve had carefully drenched the campfire but moonlight cast an eerie glow through the swaying jack pine and aspen. The wind rattled the guy ropes and snapped the fabric of the tent. Aster watched finger-like branches trail across the roof. She heard footsteps and then someone digging around in the doused campfire. Had someone seen a spark?

Curiously, she unzipped the tent and stuck her head out. A figure bent over the ashes, stirring them with a stick. He was a short man with a floppy hat and a long coat. She suppressed a giggle. Steve was obviously trying to have some fun with the tourists.

She heard a zipper and glanced away. Steve emerged from his tent and zipped it shut behind him. Aster looked back toward the fire pit. There was no one there.

Chapter Three

When breakfast ended, everyone helped with cleanup. The campers took down the tents and packed them in their waterproof cases.

"I swear," said Aster as the group gathered around the cold campfire. "It was a short man with a floppy hat and a long coat."

Beth looked at Laurel and rolled her eyes. Did Aster always have to be the center of attention?

"We'll leave about ten o'clock," said Steve. "If you want to go for a swim, take pictures, or hike go ahead. Just wear your safety whistles and compasses and don't go too far. It is incredibly easy to get lost out here. Take readings wherever you go."

Beth saw Aster frown, examine her compass, and then stuff it in her pocket. She probably didn't even remember how it worked. What had she done all those years in Guides? The girl could barely find herself around a mall.

"The sun's too bright for any decent shots around the castle now," said Aster. "I'll probably do better in the shady forest. I should have gotten up earlier, I guess." Beth watched her walk slowly into the bush, looking for subjects.

Beth sat down on the grass, unlaced her shoes, and pulled off her socks.

Ted and Maxine found a grassy spot by the beach and stretched out in the sunshine, her head resting on his arm. Rebekkah and Steve began preparing for departure, checking for garbage and lashing bags to the canoes. Matt found a shady spot, pulled out his I-pod, and popped in his ear buds.

"I'm going for a swim," said Beth as she stretched, flexing her muscles.

"How do you know there aren't leeches?" asked Laurel as she dug out her e-book reader.

"Every lake has leeches," said Beth. "I didn't get any last night so this probably is a pretty good spot for swimming. Why don't you come with me?"

"You just told me every lake has leeches and now you expect me to come with you!" said Laurel. She stretched her wide mouth into a grimace, sat down on the grass, and crossed her legs.

Beth looked down at her and grinned. "Wuss."

"I'm going to lie in the shade and read for a while. We'll be getting enough exercise and sun soon enough." Laurel looked off toward the bush. "I hope Aster doesn't get lost. She didn't seem to get the orienteering lessons very well."

"If she does," said Beth as she scratched her head making her ultra short brown hair Stand up on end, "I'm sure everyone will rush around in a panic until she's safe."

"What's up with you?" asked Laurel. "You've been a bear for months and you've given nothing but attitude this whole trip."

"Sorry, I didn't mean to ruin it for you." Beth bit the inside of her lip and looked out over the lake. "I shouldn't have come."

"This is the last time the Power Triangle will be together before we all head off in different directions," said Laurel. "I wanted it to be a good memory for all of us." She patted the grass beside her.

Beth sighed and sat down. "I only came to be with you," said Beth. "I'm sick to death of perfect little Aster and her perfect little life."

"Jeez," said Laurel. "You won a full athletic scholarship to Boston University. Your life looks pretty good right now. Aster's going to be living with her parents while she goes to school."

"What a tragedy that will be," said Beth. "Perfect mommy and daddy, with perfect little sister, in their perfect home, with her perfect boyfriend taking her out every weekend."

"Woah," said Laurel. "Where is all this coming from? Why are you jealous of Aster? I thought she was your friend. Are you jealous when something good happens to me?"

"No, of course not."

"Then why are you jealous of Aster?"

"Come on," said Beth. "Even you must be tired of how easy things are for her. And when she has the least bit of trouble with anything, she pulls that dreamy lost lamb look and everyone rushes to her rescue."

"You're exaggerating," said Laurel. "Besides, we all rush to each other's rescue. We're the Power Triangle. Aster would help you if you asked. It's not her fault if you don't."

Beth blew air slowly through her partially opened lips. "She has everything, even the hottest boyfriend."

Laurel's brow furrowed as she studied Beth's long face. "Do you have a thing for him?"

Beth yanked out a blade of grass, then another, and another. "I did. But he never looked twice at me once he spotted angel-face Aster."

"Ah, Jeez. I'm sorry. Did Aster know?"

Beth shook her head.

"Well, then you can't blame her for anything."

"I know," said Beth.

Laurel reached over and squeezed her hand. "I know it's been tough since your mom, you know."

"Yeah, it has," said Beth as she twirled a green blade between her thumb and finger. "I'll be glad to get out of that house. Dad's been a hopeless drunk ever since. Maybe he was before, I can't remember. The house is falling down around us and he just sits there. Useless."

Laurel wrapped her arm around Beth. "So take a break from it all. Relax and try to have some fun. Look at this cool place." She gestured toward the castle looming over them. "Even if it is a little *Psycho.*

"I gotta say," said Beth. "I'm really impressed with this Jimmy McOuat. He knew how to make a house."

"I guess," said Laurel. "I keep expecting Norman Bates to look out one of those windows."

Beth remembered the silhouette she had seen upon their arrival. She shook off the spider-like tickle travelling down her spine.

"I think my old man would fit right in here," said Beth.

"I'm sorry," whispered Laurel.

"Did you know Aster's parents are putting in a swimming pool?" said Beth. "A pool for God's sake. Aster barely likes swimming. She says she gets too sunburned. What I wouldn't do to have my own swimming pool."

Beth nodded. "I'm sure her life isn't as perfect as it seems. No one's is."

"Sorry," said Beth. "I know you got your own problems."

Laurel gave a smile that lit up her whole face. "Who me?"

"Have you seen your dad lately?"

"He dropped by for about ten minutes on my birthday," said Laurel.

Beth thought for a moment. "That was months ago."

"Yeah, I guess he's busy with his real family," said Laurel.

"That sucks."

"Yeah, but mom's latest boyfriend is putting in a hot-tub so when we come home for Christmas we can sit outside in steaming bubbles and watch the snow fall. It's not a swimming pool but at least we can use it in the winter. She'll probably have booted him out by then and we can have it all to ourselves."

Beth laughed. "She does go through a lot of men."

"But not until they do something useful for her," said Laurel with a tilt of her head. "The last one overhauled the engine on the car. The one before that built a deck. I honestly wonder if she goes through the yellow pages to pick out her next victim."

They both laughed.

"Families," said Beth. "It's a shame we can't pick 'em."

"We can pick our friends," said Laurel. "And good friends are priceless."

Beth nodded. "I know. Sometimes I'm just a jealous old bitch."

Laurel nodded, her red hair bobbing around her wide smile. "Sometimes we all are. If it'll make you feel any better, Aster had to have a wart removed last month."

Beth burst into a raucous laugh. "A little," she admitted. "Now go read your silly romance."

"How do you know it's a silly romance?" asked Laurel.

"Is it a romance?" asked Beth as she stood.

"Yeah."

"Then it's silly."

Laurel punched her gently in the calf. "Cripes, it's like punching a tree. No wonder you won a scholarship."

Beth laughed as she stripped off her shirt and pants, revealing her swimsuit underneath. Her arms and legs were thick with muscle. Her stomach was tight and flat. She dropped her clothes in a pile beside Laurel and jogged to the lake.

* * * * *

Laurel watched her friend swim for a while, and then lost herself in the Scottish moors with the rakish count and his unfortunate bride. Time passed without notice.

"Where's your friend?" asked Steve as he looked down at Laurel stretched out on her side. The angle exaggerated his already long nose. He looked like the less attractive younger brother of Jeff Goldblum with shorter hair.

Laurel sat up and looked toward the lake. "Swimming, I thought."

"Not Beth," he said. "She's getting changed. Aster. I sent Matt to get her quite a while ago."

Laurel stood up and looked around. "I have no idea."

Chapter Four

Steve looked at his watch. "It's twenty after ten. I told everyone we were leaving at ten."

"I'm sure she'll be along any minute," said Laurel. She hoped Aster wasn't going to stir things up. She turned as Beth approached. "Have you seen Aster?"

Beth shook her head. Rebekkah, Maxine, and Ted were waiting by the canoes. "Did you ask them?" She nodded her head toward the others.

"They haven't seen her," said Steve.

"She's never late," said Beth. "Her family runs like clockwork. It's like a major sin to keep someone waiting. Aster can be early but never late."

Matt emerged from the bush carrying Aster's camera. He walked toward them, turning it over in his hands. "Isn't this—"

"Aster's camera," said Laurel. Her bright grey eyes widened as she exchanged a look with Beth. Her stomach did an uncomfortable twist.

"Where did you find it?" asked Steve.

"A little ways into the bush, not far from the castle. It's pretty dirty. I called her name several times but there was no response. I found a trail and followed it. No Aster. I did find this huge pile of animal bones though. I think someone's been killing the wildlife."

"But this is parkland!" said Laurel.

"Yeah, something's not right. There were all kinds of bones, fairly fresh. I figured she stopped to take some pictures and then put the camera down and forgot it."

"No way," said Beth. "She'd never lose that. It's like her third arm."

"Then what the hell happened and where is she?" said Steve.

"Maybe she caught someone poaching," said Beth.

They broke into two search parties: Rebekkah, Maxine, and Ted, made one group, and Steve, Beth, and Laurel made the other. Matt stayed behind. He told Ted the bearing he had travelled. Steve decided they should go a little farther into the bush on the same path.

"My satellite phone's in my pack already in the canoe," said Rebekkah to Matt. "Use it if you need to. If Aster is badly injured, they can send in a helicopter."

Rebekkah's group went behind the castle and into the woods while Steve's stayed parallel to the front door, each group following a rough path. Before entering the woods, Steve took out his compass and noted the bearing. They were fairly sure Aster had gone in one of those two directions. The forest was too thick everywhere else.

When Steve's party reached the animal bones, they stopped. On the left side of the path skulls, leg bones, wings, mammal spines, fish bones, and feet were carelessly tossed into the bush, forming a rough pile.

"That's a beaver skull," said Steve pointing to its large front teeth. "I think that's rabbit and a partridge."

"Nothing very big," said Laurel. "No deer or moose. Lots of fish. There's even some rodent skulls here. I recognize them from our fieldtrips to Kingfisher Lake."

She looked at Beth, who nodded in confirmation. It had been one of the best memories of the Power Triangle. For three days, they had shared a cabin, cooking on an open fire, netting critters in the lake and examining them under microscopes, pulling apart and sorting the tiny bones in owl pellets, and playing the survival game with a compass and map. Aster had been terrible, unable to get the hang of lining her compass up with north, taking a reading, and walking in the right direction. However, no one could cook like her over an open fire.

"Those were good times," whispered Beth.

"I hope she hasn't gone very far," said Laurel.

"The hunter probably doesn't have a gun," said Steve examining the bones. "I don't see any bullet holes."

"Bow and arrow?" asked Laurel as she kicked a tiny skull.

Steve shook his head. "I don't think so."

"Maybe he's a trapper then," said Beth.

Steve nodded.

"Or uses a slingshot," suggested Laurel.

"Yeah, that would work too." He looked around the woods. "Slingshots can be deadly and they're silent. Keep alert."

"Why?" Beth chewed on a strand of hair. "Do you think this hunter, or trapper, or whatever, took Aster? Do you think he's dangerous?"

Steve shrugged his thin shoulders. "I don't know. To the best of my knowledge, no one should be killing anything out here. I don't understand what's going on. Just keep your eyes and ears open." He scratched his scruffy chin, thinking.

There really wasn't a trail, not the kind they had been using for portages anyway. Animals had created a rough path through the woods toward the lake but it didn't seem to come from anywhere specific. Bugs hummed in the warming air and the thrum of a partridge sounded in the distance. The smell of cedar, pine, and Labrador tea filled the forest as they stepped over rocks, limbs, and the occasional rotting trunk. Steve went first, careful not to let branches swing back and hit Beth behind him. Laurel brought up the rear, frequently looking back to be sure they weren't followed. Sweat formed on their foreheads and trickled down their backs.

After twenty minutes, any resemblance to a trail disappeared. Steve stopped walking and the girls stared into the shady woods. A white-throated sparrow called, "Oh sweet Canada Canada Canada." A small yellow butterfly drunkenly flew around them twice and then fluttered away.

Steve took out his compass and made another reading. "We'd better head back. Aster wouldn't have kept going without a trail. She must have gone in a different direction."

"The other group probably found her by now," said Laurel.

Beth bit her lip and gave a small nod.

The way back seemed to take forever. Laurel shuddered when they again passed the pile of bones. Something bright further in the bush caught her eye.

"Wait," she said and left the trail. A wave of fear passed through her gut as she picked up a yellow whistle on a lanyard and held it up for the others to see. "It's Aster's whistle."

When the castle wall came into view, they increased their pace, anxious to see Aster waiting with Matt and the others.

Matt, however, wasn't there.

"Our packs!" said Laurel as she pointed toward the canoes.

The packs, which Steve and Rebekkah had been in the process of lashing, were opened and the contents strewn about the beach. The group walked toward the water. Laurel gathered up packaged dried fruit, a first aid kit, a white bottle of sunscreen, and an orange spray can of insect repellent.

"What the hell?" said Beth as she picked up her grey T-shirt.

Voices and the sounds of bush being disturbed drew their attention away from the mess on the beach. Around the corner of the castle came Rebekkah, Maxine, and Ted. They were carrying Matt. Ted had his arms and Maxine and Rebekkah each had a leg. Rebekkah's hands were red and blood dripped from Matt's right leg. They gently lowered him onto the grass.

"We need a first aid kit," shouted Rebekkah.

Laurel dropped the fruit, sunscreen, and insect repellent and rushed over with the white box emblazoned with a red cross. "What happened?" She passed the kit to Rebekkah who knelt beside Matt and pulled off his hiking boots.

Rebekkah began to unsnap his jeans. "Sorry, Matt," she said. "No time for modesty. I have to see how bad it is." She pulled his jeans down over his slim hips and muscular thighs. In different circumstances, Laurel would appreciate this chance to take a peek but when Matt cried out in pain as the jeans passed over his injured calf, her stomach took another twist. His blond hair was soaked with sweat and he held his arm over his face, blocking out the sun.

Beth swore as the damaged leg was revealed.

"It was an animal trap," said Maxine, wheezing. "With teeth."

"Out here?" Steve's face scrunched up with anger.

Maxine nodded, then dug out her puffer and took a long pull.

Ted wandered over to the canoes and started to pick up the scattered supplies. "What happened here?"

"We don't know," said Laurel. What the hell was going on? This didn't look like an animal's foraging. Numerous knots, zippers, and buttons had been undone.

Rebekkah, who had worked as a paramedic, quickly cleaned the leg wound and wrapped it in a bandage. "We have to get him to a hospital," she said, "and report this to the MNR. We all need to leave, now. We'll call for a helicopter. Ted, bring my phone from the front pocket of my pack. We'll move Matt into the shade until help comes."

"Why did you leave camp?" asked Beth as she bent to help Matt to his feet. Steve took his other side. Matt hooked his arms over their shoulders and hopped toward a tall birch. He gasped from the pain and then answered, his voice thin and weak. "I thought I heard Aster call out. I followed her shout into the bush. Then it seemed farther away. I took a few steps off the trail and bam." He swore.

Ted called out, "Set Matt down. We have a problem."

Matt sank onto the stones, grateful to stop moving.

"What now?" asked Steve. He wiped the sweat from his high forehead and prominent nose with the back of his arm.

"The phone is missing."

"No," said Rebekkah. "Let me look."

She went over and rummage through what was left in her pack. Then she stood up, put her hands on her hips and said, "and one of the canoes has a hole in it. It will fill with water."

"What?" Steve went to look.

Rebekkah and Beth followed. Two sharp edge slices formed a V-shape in the bottom of Aster and Matt's canoe.

Rebekkah frowned. "It looks like a bear clawed the bottom open."

"It looks more like someone cut it with an axe or a knife," said Beth.

They all looked at each other.

"I think it's safe to say it wasn't one of us. Matt was the only one alone and, considering what's happened to him, the last thing he would want would be to be trapped here."

"What are we going to do?" Maxine's voice rose. "We've got to get out of here!" She stopped, overcome by coughing, and then took another pull on her puffer. Ted went to her and rubbed her back, whispering soothing phrases. The group gathered around Maxine.

"Well," said Steve, "it's clear we need to get Matt out immediately.

"And Maxine," said Ted. "I'm worried she's heading into a full asthma attack."

"Agreed," said Rebekkah. "But somebody has to stay behind."

Chapter Five

"What does that mean?" asked Beth, her hands on her hips. No one was going to be left behind if she had anything to say about it.

"What if Aster comes back and we're all gone?" asked Steve.

Beth flinched. The thought of little Aster alone and frightened, maybe even hurt, gave her a pain in the chest. She wished she didn't care, but she did.

"Besides," said Rebekkah. "Our canoes aren't really made for three. We'd have to leave all our stuff behind as well."

"Who cares about stuff?" said Laurel. "You can't leave us here alone."

"Of course not," said Steve. "I'll stay with you."

"Oh," said Beth. "I guess that's okay then." She gave Laurel a comforting smile.

Steve continued. "Rebekkah will take Matt in her canoe and Ted will take Maxine. They'll take the shortest route possible to where Ted can get a signal on his cell phone." He looked at Ted. "You've still got your phone?" Ted patted his chest pocket and nodded. "Ted will call for Medivac and also inform them of our situation. Help will be here before you know it."

Maxine took another inhale of her puffer. Her breathing was still far from normal. Ted reassured her and rubbed her back. As the two canoes pushed off from the shore, Laurel reached over and took Beth's hand. They watched until the canoes were out of sight.

"What about Aster?" said Laurel. "Do we keep looking for her?"

"We should have a good lunch first," said Steve. "I'm also thinking if we light a fire, she might see the smoke and be able to make her way back. Honestly, she's probably just lost. It's very easy to do out here."

"I doubt it," said Beth. "Someone ransacked and sabotaged our canoes."

"Maybe it was a bear," said Laurel hopefully.

"A bear who likes to pile the bones of his meals in one spot and managed to avoid a big metal trap while doing that?"

"Come on," said Steve. "Let's get a big fire going. I'll make some coffee and we'll have lunch. Everything looks worse on an empty stomach."

Lunch turned out to be macaroni and tuna casserole and peas. Beth wondered about the wisdom of heating up tuna if the vandal *had* been a rogue bear.

Laurel shared more information on Jimmy McOuat. Then she lowered the booklet and looked from Steve's face to Beth's. "Aster said she saw Jimmy's ghost last night. We all laughed at her but maybe she was telling the truth. I've never known her to tell an outright lie like that."

"You think a ghost tore apart the packs and damaged the canoe?" asked Beth. "That seems rather Christopher Pike." They sat cross-legged on the grass around the campfire.

"Not a ghost, a person. Aster just thought it was Jimmy McOuat because we were talking about him before bed. It could have been anyone," said Laurel.

"That's true," said Steve. "There have been a number of odd hermits living in the north over the decades. One could have moved into the area."

"But his clothes," said Beth. "She said he had a floppy hat and a long coat, like Jimmy."

"It could have been a raincoat and a sun hat that got a little worse for wear," said Steve.

"Yeah, that's right," said Laurel.

"Okay," said Beth as she scraped the last of her tuna salad out of her bowl. "So, it's not a bear and it's not a ghost. It's just a crazy hermit."

Laurel frowned. "Nobody said crazy."

"Right," said Beth. "He just trashes people's stuff for no reason but he's not crazy."

Steve stood up. "I think he set that bear trap."

"What?" said Beth, also standing up. "To catch a bear or to catch us?"

"I don't know," said Steve. "But I've never heard of anyone setting traps here. Besides, that was a very old trap. Those types aren't even legal anymore."

"Why didn't you say that before the other canoes left?" asked Beth.

"I didn't want to worry my wife," he admitted. "She needed to focus on Matt and Maxine. I can take care of myself."

"Well, that's nice," said Laurel. "Can you take care of us too?"

"We just have to stay together until help arrives," he said. "Search and rescue will be here before dark. They'll find Aster. It'll all work out." He picked up the bucket of water beside the campfire and set it on the burning embers to heat. "We'll wash up the dishes and try to keep busy until then."

"Shouldn't we continue looking for Aster? asked Laurel.

"I don't want to risk anyone else stepping into a trap," said Steve. "We'll leave it to the professionals."

Laurel gave Beth a worried glance. Beth sat back down and shrugged. There didn't seem to be anything else they could do.

* * * * *

Laurel read through the information she had brought on Jimmy McOuat. "You know he probably wouldn't have built this castle in the woods if his prospecting had been a success."

"Prospecting?" said Beth. "I thought you said he was a farmer."

"He was for a while," said Laurel. "And very successful too. He owned three properties. Then he got gold fever and sold everything. He wound up with nothing. In the end, he came here and built a little shack on crown land."

"Not the castle?"

"Not at first."

"Do you think he built it for a woman?"

"Maybe. Some say he built it for a woman named Jane that he hoped to marry. But, in the end, he died alone. Drowned in the winter. His fishing net snagged a button on his coat and pulled him in. They didn't find him until spring."

"Sad and creepy," said Beth.

Laurel watched Steve as he filled the basin with cold water from the lake and added a dash of bleach. Periodically, he glanced in their direction and then looked quickly away. She saw him surreptitiously watching the woods. "There's something you're not telling us," she said.

Beth looked sharply at her and then at their guide. "Laurel knows people," said Beth. "If you're trying to keep a secret, give it up."

Steve slipped on an oven mitt and lifted the bucket of steaming water off the coals. He squeezed a dribble of dish soap into the water and gave it a vigorous stir. The girls handed him their dishes.

"Well?" said Laurel. She crossed her arms. This was no time for additional mysteries.

"Okay," said Steve. "I just remembered something I heard on the news in the spring. Some investor from Ignace disappeared. Rumour was he'd lost all his money. The bank took his house. Then his fiancé left town without him."

"Kinda like Jimmy McOuat," said Laurel. "But I doubt this investor went off into the woods to build a castle."

Steve nodded. "I remember his first name. It was James."

Beth swore. "I've got a bad feeling about this," she said.

"Me too," said Laurel.

Steve washed and rinsed the dishes. Laurel dried and Beth put them away. The sun beat down and the cry of a hawk underscored the sense of isolation. Steve threw more sticks on the fire.

What Laurel wouldn't give for a satellite phone. Why had she talked the others into going on this trip without bringing one? At least they hadn't come alone. That had been the original idea but three in a canoe didn't seem workable. It had made more sense to join up with others. Then Aster, always worried about getting lost, had suggested they go with a guide. Beth had agreed. Laurel suspected it was to avoid too much intimate contact with Aster.

In retrospect, that was a good idea. If they had come alone, who knows what might have happened? There would be no one to wait behind in case Aster returned. Poor Aster. Where was she? Had she stepped into another bear trap? Was she bleeding to death somewhere, unconscious and not able to call for help? What if they never saw her again?

A scream came from the tower! All three jumped to their feet.

"Stay here," ordered Steve.

"No way," said Beth.

Laurel grabbed her arm. "Don't go, please. Stay with me."

Laurel looked from her to Steve's back as he jogged toward the castle. She sighed and nodded. Together they moved at an angle slowly toward the castle and the beach, in order to see the tower clearly. The sound of feet on wood, creaking and groaning, came from inside. Beth hoped none of the logs would collapse on Steve. Hadn't he said the stairs were in pieces?

A moment later, Beth pointed. "Look, the top window facing the lake."

Steve's shape appeared in the opening. There were loud voices, two men's and a woman's. But, they could not make out the words. A second figure, with a floppy hat appeared in the window. Steve raised his fist and punched at the figure. The other man punched back. Steve stumbled, hit the window sill, and flipped out the opening. He gave a cry of terror as he plunged four stories toward the ground.

It's not so far, he'll be okay, Laurel told herself as he cart wheeled down. Then his head hit the side of the tower, snapping his neck. He thudded to the grass. A figure peered out the window and then stepped away as the girls ran to Steve.

There was no blood, but his head was twisted at an odd angle. His eyes were open, staring off toward the beach.

"Steve, Steve," cried Laurel as she bent beside him, her red hair falling over her face. She put her head on his chest. No heartbeat. "Help me move him. I have to do rescue breathing!"

As they straightened out his body, the bones in his neck crunched. Laurel tasted bile in the back of her throat. She told herself not to throw up.

"Don't," said Beth. "If you bring him back, he'll be in agony. His neck is badly broken. How can we keep him alive until help comes? You'll just make him suffer for nothing."

Laurel sat back on her bottom. "I don't think I could anyway. It feels like some of his ribs are broken too. And there's blood in his mouth."

"Internal damage," said Beth.

"Yeah, more than we could fix with our first aid kit." Laurel gently closed his eyes. She looked up at Beth. "I think Aster's up there."

They both stood and stared at the tower's top window.

Laurel asked, "What do you want to do?"

"I don't think we have a choice," said Beth as she took her friend's hand. "Triangle Power."

Chapter Six

Laurel looked at her friend in shock. Was this the same girl who couldn't wait to leave Aster behind in Thunder Bay and head off to Boston without looking back?

"If Steve couldn't stop him," said Laurel, "what makes you think we can? Now that we know where she is, wouldn't it be better to head out in the canoe and reach the rescue party. We can tell them what's going on. If we all get killed, there will be no one to tell them anything."

"And what if Aster is gone again when we get back? What if they never find her?" asked Beth. "Do you want that on your conscience?"

"No," said Laurel. "Of course not. But I don't think Aster wants us to get ourselves killed either."

"Is there another way out of the tower?" asked Beth. "The least we can do is block the exits so he can't escape."

"I don't know."

"No floor plan in that info pack you brought?"

Laurel shook her head no. They both looked up toward the tower again. They heard Aster shouting and a man replying, but they couldn't understand the words.

"She's not making it easy for him anyway," said Beth. "Good for her."

"When we get home," said Laurel, "her parents are never going to let her out of their sight."

Beth nodded thoughtfully. "They kinda are helicopter parents, eh?"

"They wouldn't let her apply to any colleges or universities outside of Thunder Bay. Her mother didn't want her to go on this trip. She said Aster was being reckless canoeing and portaging for five days just before the start of university." Laurel thought of how her own parents always encouraged her to take sensible risks, to stretch her wings. They often said she could do whatever she set her mind to. What must it be like to have parents who do everything for you, the underlying message being that you're too helpless or incompetent to do it yourself?

"Maybe there are worse things than having a father who barely notices you," said Beth. She took a deep breath. "We're not going off in the canoe. We're going to go inside that castle and see what's what. Are you with me?"

Laurel's heart leapt into her throat, but she took Beth's hand and said, "Triangle Power forever."

Cautiously they crept under the sagging roof of the porch/awning. The four logs holding up the roof were solid, but the cross pieces supporting the shingles were cracked and rotting.

They stared into the dark interior of the main house. It was as big as a barn. Inside, beams crisscrossed in all directions, like the last sticks in a Ker Plunk game. Sunbeams trickled in through the glassless windows spotlighting dust, insects, and floating spores. Bits of grass and weed poked up through the floor boards.

"It looks like there's only one way up the tower," said Beth as she pointed toward a broken and slanting staircase.

"We could sit at the bottom and shout up to tell Aster we're here," suggested Laurel.

Beth looked thoughtful. "What do you think he might do to her up there?"

"I don't know," admitted Laurel. "Are you worried he might push her out the window?"

"I think that was an accident. But why has he taken her?" asked Beth.

"Lonely, like the real Jimmy, I guess."

"But why her? Haven't there been lots of other people passing through over the summer?"

Laurel wondered if Beth was on to something. What had triggered this James to react and take Aster? Was it simply because she was alone, small, and vulnerable. An easy pick? Or was there something about her?

"Wait," she said. "I read about the woman he was supposed to marry. Her name was Jane. She was smart, attractive, and a good housekeeper and . . ." Laurel bit her lip concentrating. "And, she sounded a little like Aster, I think. That's it! Aster probably looks like Jane, the woman he was supposed to marry."

"Hold on," said Beth as they stood in the dark, watching the staircase. "That's the real Jimmy. What about this one? What did his fiancé look like?"

"How am I supposed to know that? But anyway, I think this guy identifies with the historical Jimmy. Maybe his fiancé looked like Jane too. Who knows? But, if he hasn't hurt her, that must mean he wants her, right?"

"I guess," said Beth. "But just how much does he *want* her?"

Laurel cringed. "Eww. You think he might...?"

"Who knows what he's capable of? He's obviously dangerous."

"What can we do?" asked Laurel.

For the second time in a short while her friend shocked her. "We can go up there and kick his sorry butt," she said.

Laurel looked at the rickety stairs. Steps were missing, some were slanted, and many were threaded with dry rot. Aster was a little thing and maybe this James was as well, but she and Beth were standard-sized women. Her curves had weight and so did Beth's muscles. Would those boards hold the both of them or would they bring the entire thing down in a four floor crash? Even if they made it to the top, what then? This guy could have weapons.

"Really?" she said. "This isn't some schoolyard bully."

"And we aren't little girls," said Beth. "Besides, I'm not talking a full frontal assault to start with anyway. I'm going to let my BFF drama girl strut her stuff."

"Huh?"

"You're going to try to talk him into letting Aster go."

"I am?"

"Just wait here while I get us some weapons for plan B," said Beth.

"Weapons, right," muttered Laurel as Beth exited through the door and out of view. The voices of Aster and James drifted down from above. They were no longer shouting. That was a good sign. She heard steps and dust drifted down through the crooked stairwell. She leaned forward and looked up. More holes in the steps gaped overhead. She jumped as Beth touched her arm.

"Jeez, wear a bell or something," she snapped.

Beth passed her a jackknife. "Keep it folded in your pocket and don't let him see it."

"God, I hope I don't have to use it."

"Me too. If he takes it away, he could use it on the both of us."

"Nice thought," said Laurel. "What do you have?"

Beth turned around and showed her a hammer tucked in her belt. Laurel imagined that muscular arm slamming a hammer into James' head. It would crack like an egg. She grimaced. It would serve him right though, for pushing Steve out of the window and kidnapping Aster. She mustn't develop sympathy for him. But, she should make him think she has.

Beth nodded and led the way. Laurel felt guilty for not going first. Beth always put herself in the point position, spearheading the Triangle. The stairs creaked and groaned as they ascended. The voices above stopped. There would be no element of surprise, if they made it to the top. She tried to place her feet exactly where Beth had. If the steps held for her friend, they were probably safe for her too.

Crack! A board under Beth snapped in half, the stairwell rocked and Beth stumbled to regain her footing. She paused ahead and looked back at Laurel. Her short hair was thick with dust. Laurel nodded. She would pass over that board.

When they reached the top, Aster and James were standing by the same window from which Steve had fallen. James held an axe in one hand and clasped Aster's shoulder with the other. Laurel's stomach did another twist at the thought of her friend cart wheeling down the side of the building and cracking her head.

The kidnapper wore a filthy large straw hat, a long raincoat open at the front, a grey sweatshirt underneath, camouflage pants, and hiking boots. His long, narrow face hadn't been washed for weeks. Matted clumps of hair jutted out from under his hat. His hands were covered in dirt and scratches. His eyes were a pale mint-blue, bloodshot and underscored by dark half-circles.

She and Beth stood side by side at the top of the stairs and looked at Aster. There was a small bump over Aster's right eye but otherwise she seemed all right. A pile of ropes lay on the floor in front of her.

"Are you okay?" Beth asked.

Aster nodded. "Yes."

The small man beside her glared at the two new arrivals. "Get out of here," he said. "Redheads. Nothing but trouble."

Beth gave Laurel a look. Laurel remembered Jimmy's written request for a bride. *Her hair may be any colour but fiery red.* Laurel turned and smiled her most dazzling at James.

"I'm Laurel, and this is Beth. We're Aster's friends."

"Who's Aster?"

Laurel blinked.

"He thinks I'm someone named Jane," said Aster.

Crazy as a loon, thought Laurel.

Chapter Seven

Beth looked from Laurel to Aster. Laurel gave her a small smile.

Either this man's fiancé had been named Jane and he was nuts thinking Aster was her, or he read about Jimmy McOuat's failed engagement and believed he was the historical Jimmy and Aster was that Jane. Therefore, a double package of nuts.

"Of course," said Laurel. "You're his fiancé. I didn't recognize you in this light."

James frowned, studying Laurel.

"Aster," said Beth. Laurel elbowed her. "I mean, Jane. What's with the ropes?"

"James tied me up, but I got free. He couldn't tie a decent knot to save his life."

Obviously Aster's acid tongue hadn't been harmed. "Oh," said Laurel with artificial excitement. "You were playing a game. Good thing you've always been good with ropes, Jane."

Increasing bewilderment showed on James' face.

"Did you say her name was Beth? She don't look like Elizabeth." He stared at Beth. "What happened to her hair?"

Laurel frantically tried to recall everything she had read about Jimmy McOuat. Beth? Elizabeth? Hair? Then she remembered. "Ah, Elizabeth McClure, your neighbour. Oh, well. It's a sad tale, Jimmy. The whole family got lice and Elizabeth had to cut her hair."

Beth gave her a doubtful look.

"Her husband, Arthur, no I mean Angus, will be along later. We've come for tea."

"Tea?" said James.

"Of course, tea," said Laurel. "You always give visitors tea. You're a gracious host. Everyone knows that."

James slowly lowered the axe. "I don't think I have any tea."

"Oh, that's all right," said Laurel with a friendly grin. "We do. It's in our packs in the canoe."

"I don't have cups."

Laurel gave a carefree laugh. "Don't worry, Jimmy. We have all that. All you need to do is get some wood for the fire. I see you have your axe, so we're all set."

James looked at the axe in his hand as though seeing it for the first time.

"Could you do that, Jimmy?" said Laurel. "Could you get some firewood and help us get the fire going for tea. I'm sure Jane would love a cup of tea. Wouldn't you Jane?'

"Yes," said Aster. "I'm very thirsty and my throat is dry."

"All right then," said James.

"Beth, Elizabeth, you go first," said Laurel. "Then I'll follow, and then Jimmy and Jane."

"Are you sure you want to turn your back on him?" whispered Beth.

Laurel waved her on. "We'll see you outside by the campfire, Jimmy."

He nodded and then looked at Aster with a confused expression.

Laurel followed Beth's quick pace down the stairs. She had spoken confidently, but she did not like the idea of James following behind her with an axe in his hand either. Although she hurried, it seemed to take forever. When she reached the bottom, Beth pulled her quickly through the main building and out the door. James and Aster's footsteps sounded coming slowly down the stairs.

Beth pushed her to the left side of the doorway. "Get out your knife," she hissed.

"What? No," said Laurel. "We can get him to put down the axe when we have tea."

"Maybe, but we'll never have a better chance than this." She took out the hammer and lifted it high.

"I don't think—"

"Shut up," ordered Beth.

Reluctantly, Laurel took out the pocket knife and opened it. Where would she stab him? In the throat? That would kill him and she wasn't a murderer. How would it feel to stab someone? Would she get blood sprayed on her? She would stab him in the upper arm. That would make him drop the axe.

Aster stepped through the door as Beth stepped forward and swung the hammer.

"No!" cried Laurel but Beth realized at the same time and stumbled to avoid hitting her friend. Laurel tried to dodge behind Aster to jab Jimmy in the arm. She realized she was on the wrong side just as her knife stabbed at his left shoulder. Because she was trying to reach over Aster, the impact was minimal, ripping his shirt and barely breaking the skin.

Beth jerked Aster forward and away from her captor. Aster took the opportunity to run toward the clearing. Before Laurel could raise her hammer to strike again, James grabbed Laurel with his left arm, twisted her wrist making her drop the knife, and pulled her tightly into his chest. He raised the sharp blade of the axe to her throat. Laurel felt the edge pressing against her skin, followed by a sharp pain, and a trickle of blood.

"Drop the hammer," said James to Beth. "Back away."

She did.

James edged forward, tightly gripping Laurel with his left arm across her breasts while holding the axe to her throat.

* * * * *

Aster reached the clearing and picked up the first suitable weapon she could find, a baseball-sized rock. She turned around and saw Beth backing away from the castle. Laurel emerged with James holding her against his chest. The axe was pressed up against Laurel's throat and Aster could see a trickle of blood on Laurel's T-shirt.

Aster put her hand holding the rock behind her back and waited. Beth came to stand beside her.

"Thanks for coming for me," said Aster. "I'm guessing that was a hard thing to decide."

"Actually," said Beth, "it was surprisingly simple."

"Triangle Power?"

"Yep."

"Looks like we need to call on it again," said Aster as James and Laurel approached. Laurel's eyes were wide and filling with tears.

"Got any ideas?" said Beth. "My last one didn't work so well."

"But you tried," said Aster."I wasn't sure you would." Laurel wasn't the only actor. "Move away. When I cough, create a diversion."

Beth nodded and took several steps to the side.

"Jimmy," Aster said. "What are you doing to our guests?"

"They attacked me," he said warily, looking from Aster to Beth and back again.

"No, you must be mistaken."

"That bitch tried to hit me with a hammer," he shouted.

Aster paused. She made her voice sweet as maple syrup. "Jimmy, that's a terrible word to use. I've never heard you use profane language before."

"Well, I . . . ."

"It's alright my sweet," she said lifting her left hand in a placating gesture. "There's been a misunderstanding."

He relaxed his grip on Laurel, his face moved to the side to look straight at her.

"What kind of misunderstanding?" he said.

Aster coughed, signalling Beth.

"I want my tea right now!" shouted Beth. She waved her arms.

Jimmy's eyes opened wide as he stared at Beth.

"You think I'll let you hurt my friend," whispered Aster. She wound up and let fly the most important pitch of her life. The rock hit James square in the left eye. He screamed, dropped the axe, and clutched his face. Laurel ran forward.

"Triangle Power," shouted Aster as she picked up another rock and whipped it at James' groin. He cried out and fell to his knees.

Laurel and Beth joined in, hurling rocks as hard as they could. A cut opened on James' cheek. Aster's next rock hit him hard in the chest. He gasped and pitched forward.

"The canoe," shouted Laurel. "Come on."

The girls raced for the water. Aster took a third paddle from the damaged canoe. Quickly they unlashed the packsacks and tent and tossed them onto the rocky shore in order to make room for a third person. They pushed the canoe half into the water. Beth piled into the stern, prepared to steer and provide power. Aster sat in the middle directly on the keel with her legs straight out in front of her, her feet tucked under Laurel's seat in the bow, and her back pressed tightly against the yoke. They back-paddled frantically through the floating straw-like burreed.

Beth swore. Aster looked past her to see James up on his feet and awkwardly running for the water.

"Unbelievable," muttered Aster. It felt as though she was watching video footage. It didn't seem real. Any second, she would click on the pause button and consider where to add the music.

"This psycho just won't quit," said Beth as she tried to steer the canoe in a circle.

James splashed through the water and weeds until he was waist deep. Then he took a long breath and submerged. The music from *Jaws* sprang into Aster's mind.

"Keep paddling," ordered Beth as she turned the canoe.

A hand shot out of the water, grabbed the side of the canoe, and pulled. The boat flipped. Aster hit the water sideways but her feet remained trapped under the front seat. The canoe rose up and came down. The gunwhale smacked her smartly in the head. She sank in darkness.

Chapter Eight

Beth was the first to surface. She saw Laurel swimming for shore and James behind Laurel. She swivelled her head. No Aster. She turned again. No black hair anywhere. She dove.

She swam in ever enlarging circles hoping Aster hadn't drifted into the weeds and out of sight.

A dark shape came into view. Aster! Unconscious and floating underwater.

Beth swam to her, scooped up the body, and brought Aster to the surface. Warm blood trickled over her hands as she held Aster's head. Aster wasn't breathing. Beth kicked with her feet propelling them toward shallower water where she immediately emptied Aster's mouth, pinched Aster's nose, pressed her mouth over her friend's, and drove air into her lungs.

She picked Aster up, grateful that her friend was small and light, and carried her onto the pebbly beach. After two more breaths, Aster coughed and vomited up water. She opened her light-umber eyes and groaned. She reached her hand up to her head and looked at the blood on her fingertips. Then she suddenly sat up.

"Where's Laurel?" she said.

Beth helped Aster to her feet and pointed. Laurel had a paddle in her hand and was using it to keep James away. She circled around the now barely smoking campfire, moving this way and that.

"She always was awesome at dodge ball," said Beth.

"I think she could use some help," said Aster as she staggered forward.

"Not you," said Beth. "You were knocked out. Stay here."

Beth jogged toward the canoes and picked up another paddle.

"Bull," called Aster as she stumbled behind her. There were no more paddles, so she dug through one of the packs on the beach and pulled out a blue nylon rope. "We'll see how good *he* is at untying knots," she called to Beth.

James looked up as the two young women approached. He gave a strangled sound and began to back away.

"We can't let him escape," said Beth. She held the paddle like a club.

The three of them followed James along the shore. He fled down the beach.

"Oh, crap," said Aster as she fell to her knees.

Beth looked behind. "Aster!" she cried and ran back. Laurel joined them.

Aster vomited onto the gravel. "I feel dizzy."

"You probably have a concussion," said Beth. "I told you to stay behind."

"Well pardon me if I don't feel comfortable being left alone, what with crazy kidnappers and all."

"She's right," said Laurel. "None of us should be left alone."

"Okay," said Beth as she helped Aster to her knees. "Maybe we should just bail out the canoe and get out of here."

"That canoe?" said Laurel. She pointed out to the lake where a red object bobbed slowly away.

"Oh, rats," said Beth. "It doesn't matter. I can swim out to get it and push it back."

"I'm sure you could," said Laurel. "Leaving me to protect vomit girl from her crazy imaginary fiancé."

"We have to get him," gasped Aster as she pulled on the girls and stumbled to her feet. "I brought rope. I'm awesome at knots. I'll tie him up and he'll never get free."

"All right," said Beth. "But we'll stay together."

Their pace slowed considerably as they helped Aster along the shore. Far ahead, they could see Jimmy still running. He reached a large boulder and scrambled on top. He paused to look back. He turned, lost his footing, fell awkwardly down onto the lower rocks, and rolled into the water.

The girls looked at each other.

"Could be a trick," said Beth.

"Impressive trick," muttered Aster. "He must have been a gymnast in one of his previous lives."

Beth laughed. She had forgotten how sardonic Aster could be. While she pounded their adversaries into submission, Aster cut them with her tongue.

They finally reached the rocks. Cautiously, they climbed on top and looked into the water. A foot broke the surface as small waves passed over it. Jimmy was face first in the lake.

"Is he dead?" asked Laurel.

They carefully climbed down onto the smaller boulders. Beth prodded the foot with her paddle.

"Let's just sit here for a few minutes and watch," said Aster. "Just to make sure he's not holding his breath. You know, we turn our backs and he suddenly rises up out of the water with a sword between his teeth."

Beth snorted a laugh. The three of them climbed back up onto the higher boulders and stared at the foot. It didn't move other than from the gentle motion of the lake.

Finally Aster said, "I guess I don't need the rope."

"I'm going in," said Beth.

"The hell you are," said Laurel. "He's dead. Let's leave him there."

"No," said Aster. "You need to watch more horror movies. If we walk away, when the rescue people come, his body will be mysteriously gone. None of us will ever feel safe camping again."

"I think that's a given anyway," said Laurel.

"Nu, uh," said Aster. "I heard Fraser Valley is a beautiful place to camp. I thought we could go there next year."

Beth gave Aster a fierce hug.

"Ow, ow, head injury here," said Aster.

Beth released her, grinned, and carefully slid off the rock into the water. She dove below the surface as Laurel and Aster held hands, barely breathing. A moment later, she broke the surface, and climbed out. She stared at her friends and slowly shook her head.

"What? What?" said Aster.

"You won't believe it."

"Give," said Laurel.

"He drowned."

"We figured that," said Aster. "Why?"

"He got tangled in a fishing net."

"Yeah, so why wouldn't . . . ?" Aster looked at Laurel.

Laurel nodded. "Yeah, just like how Jimmy McOuat died."

Beth went back to the castle and found the jack knife by the castle door. Using this, she cut Jimmy free of the net. She walked through the water, towing his body behind her by his hood his bluish face up, as the other two walked along the shore. Then they pulled his body up onto the beach.

"What about Steve?" asked Laurel.

When they approached his body, two huge ravens were pecking at his face. Aster screamed in fury and stumbled toward them. They cawed in protest, flapping their wings and refusing to move until the other two girls also ran up.

"They were almost as big as you," said Beth.

"He tried to save me," said Aster. "I couldn't get to the window fast enough to catch him."

"He would have taken you with him," said Beth. "He weighs about a hundred pounds more than you."

Aster frowned and smoothed a wisp of brown hair off Steve's long forehead. "How can we protect him from the animals?"

"I have an idea," said Laurel.

They carried Steve's body to the beach, stopping often to rest. He was heavy and they were exhausted as their adrenalin dissipated. They laid him out on the stones. Laurel unrolled their tent and dragged it over the body.

"We need rocks to weigh it down," said Aster, "so the wind won't blow it away or the birds get under the tent."

"I know," said Laurel. "Jimmy McOuat's grave."

"Oh my God, we can't bury him," said Beth.

"No," said Laurel. "After the loggers destroyed all the flowers on Jimmy's grave, his friends made a cross on it with white rocks and then a circle around it. We could use those rocks."

"Not sure I'm up to that," said Aster as she sank onto the pebbles.

"You rest," said Beth. "We'll do it."

"I'm sick of feeling useless," said Aster.

"Useless," said Laurel. "If you hadn't hit James in the eye with that rock, he would have cut my throat."

"I guess," said Aster.

"We're a team," said Beth. "The Power Triangle. Without you, what are we?"

"Pretty much a line segment," said Aster. They laughed. "All right, I'll rest. I'm feeling pretty woozy anyway."

There were more than enough rocks to surround Steve's body and hold the tent down securely.

"What about James?" said Laurel. "We don't have any more rocks."

"Let them eat him," said Aster.

Laurel and Beth looked uncomfortably at each other.

"We could put the canoe on top of him," said Laurel. That might keep him cool and keep some of the animals away."

"I'm guessing you mean the one with the hole," said Beth, "and not that one." She pointed down the beach to where their good canoe was bobbing in the pondweed.

Laurel gave a squeal and high-fived Beth. Beth walked down to the good canoe, towed it back through the shallow water, pulled it up onto the beach.

Then Beth and Laurel laid the damaged canoe over James. Aster was lying on the gravel, her arm over her eyes.

"You okay?" said Laurel.

"I'm seeing double," said Aster, "and I'm having a hard time staying awake.

"I don't think we should take her in the canoe," said Beth. "It will just make it difficult for the rescuers to find us."

"But we could meet them sooner," said Laurel.

"We don't know how they're coming," said Beth. "We'd better stay put and keep her awake. If she goes to sleep, she might never wake up again."

Chapter Nine

"I can hear you," said Aster. "I'm not dead yet."

Laurel cringed and gave Beth a worried look. What if Aster had a blood clot on the brain or something? "She should probably have some water to drink," said Laurel.

"Now, that's an idea," said Aster. "I haven't had anything to drink since breakfast. What happened to the tea Laurel promised me and Jimmy?"

Her friends sat her up and put a packsack behind her back for support. Aster's hands trembled as she tried to drink the cup of water. Beth steadied it for her, a frown on her face.

Laurel studied Aster's face. Aster was always pale but her complexion had a strange grey tinge. Maybe this trip really was going to be the end of the Power Triangle. She bit her lip, feeling powerless now.

"So what happened to you on the trail, anyway?" asked Beth.

Laurel nodded. It was a good idea to keep Aster talking. That way she wouldn't fall asleep.

"I found this weird pile of animal bones," said Aster.

"Yeah, we saw that. That's where Matt found your camera."

"Matt," said Aster. "I forgot about Matt and Rebekkah. Ted and Maxine. Are they looking for me or what?"

Laurel explained what happened.

"Poor Matt," said Aster. "His girlfriend is going to be pretty upset when she gets back from Paris."

"Girlfriend?" said Beth at the same time that Laurel said, "Paris?"

"Yeah, Matt said she went for some summer school exchange program. That's why he joined his sister and Ted for the trip. I've always wanted to go to Paris, so I asked him lots about the program. It's for university students. I'd love to take pictures of the Eiffel Tower."

"That's what you were talking so much about?" asked Beth. "I thought you were hitting on him."

"No," said Aster. "He mentioned his girlfriend on the first day, so that was that. Not that it wouldn't be nice, though."

"But you have a boyfriend already," said Laurel.

Aster sighed. "No, I don't. He decided to go away for university instead of staying in Thunder Bay. He also decided this would be a good chance to meet other girls."

"Oh, that scum," said Beth. She gave Aster's hand a squeeze.

"I'm really tired," said Aster. "Couldn't I just have a little nap?" She slid her body forward until her head rested on the packsack.

"No, no," said Laurel, tugging at her. "You have to stay awake."

"Kay, but let me lie down."

Laurel frowned and looked at Beth who gave a helpless shrug.

"You were telling us about what happened to you," said Beth. "You know, when Jimmy/James kidnapped you."

"Jimmy/James?" said Aster.

"The kidnapper guy," said Beth. "James."

"James who?" muttered Aster.

"The guy lying under the canoe," said Laurel.

"Why would someone be lying under a canoe?" muttered Aster. "That can't be comfortable."

"Aster," said Laurel. "I think you should have another drink of water. Aster. Aster!"

"Oh my God," said Beth. "What are we going to do?' She shook Aster's limp shoulder and then burst into tears, covering her face with her hands.

This alarmed Laurel almost as much as Aster loosing consciousness. Beth cried less often than giant meteors struck the earth. She looked from one friend to the other. Why had she dragged them on this stupid trip? She looked at the overturned canoe and Steve's body under the unrolled tent surrounded by rocks. What would they cover Aster's body with?

Foofoofoofoofoofoo came the sound. Laurel looked out over the lake and started to cry as well. "Look, Beth, look," she said, peeling her friend's hands from her face. "It's a Search and Rescue helicopter."

* * * * *

As Beth and Laurel stepped into the hospital elevator, Laurel swore she wouldn't cry. In the morning they were both leaving for their respective universities. Aster was due to be released tomorrow but Laurel wouldn't be here to see her safely home.

"Did you see Aster's yearbook picture in the paper?" Laurel asked. "I wonder who gave it to them."

"I doubt it was Aster, or her parents," said Beth. "It's not the most flattering picture."

"Yeah," said Laurel, "but she does look a lot like James' fiancé's picture."

"I guess. But who knows if the paper photoshopped the other woman's picture?"

"I never thought of that," said Laurel. "You think they'd do that?'

Beth shrugged.

"Well, Aster is certainly the center of attention again and she did have to be rescued, just like you said."

"Don't say that!" said Beth, her forehead pulled into creases. "I'm sure Aster would have preferred to just have a nice holiday. It's not like she asked for all this trouble."

Laurel tried not to look stunned as the elevator doors opened. "No, she didn't. A lot of what happens to Aster seems to be pushed on her by other people."

"Yeah," said Beth. "I see that now."

When they entered Aster's room, she was aimlessly flipping through TV channels. She smiled and clicked off the television. "Hey you two," she said.

Both Beth and Laurel apologized repeatedly for having to leave before Aster got out of the hospital. Neither would be able to visit for long.

"Ah," said Aster, "you both came this afternoon. I said you didn't have to come back tonight."

"I wanted to say goodbye," said Laurel.

"I'm not saying goodbye," said Beth. "Just, see you later, alligator."

"After while, crocodile," said Aster.

"Pretty soon, baboon," said Laurel.

They all laughed.

"Remember when we thought that was the coolest goodbye ever?" said Beth.

"It was," said Laurel, "when we were seven."

Aster pointed to the newspaper her mother had brought. Ghost *of Jimmy McOuat Haunts Castle* read the headline. "Did you see this?"

"Yeah," said Laurel, "it's all over the news. I guess this is our fifteen minutes of fame."

"I'm glad I got my camera back," said Aster. "I might be able to sell some of the shots before the story cools off. This could be a way to get my name out there."

"My mom said maybe James was Jimmy reincarnated," said Laurel. "She's dating some guy who's into past lives and crystals. He's rearranging all the furniture according to Feng Shui. I never know where the heck anything is."

Beth and Aster laughed.

"I guess you saw the pictures on page three?" said Beth.

"Yeah," said Aster. "I'd like to punch whoever gave them that yearbook photo. I look like I'm twelve."

"I didn't think you looked much like James' ex-fiancé," said Beth.

"Thanks for that," said Aster. "She looks like a sour old grump."

"She's probably ticked off at whoever gave them her picture," said Laurel.

Aster nodded. "Well, that would be something else we had in common."

The girls chatted about plans for next year and news from friends.

"I told my parents I want to go to Paris next summer," said Aster. "They almost stroked out on me."

"It might have been a good idea to wait until you were out of the hospital before springing that on them," said Beth.

"It wouldn't matter. They'll keep me at home until they die if they can. I have to get out."

"Hey, I thought we were going camping next summer," said Laurel.

"Naw," said Beth. "We can't wait that long to get together. I was thinking we should all go skiing at Christmas."

"Yeah, I guess I'll be renewing my ski hill memberships," said Aster. "It won't be much fun without my BFFs though."

"Not here," said Beth. "Somewhere far, far away."

"Really?" said Aster.

"You bet," said Beth. "I'll arrange the whole thing. Are you in?"

"Absolutely," said Aster.

"Totally," said Laurel.

"This is one friendship that is going to stay strong," said Beth.

"Triangle Power forever," said Aster as she high-fived the other two.

Author's Note

White Otter Castle is a real place built exactly as described in the story. I have taken some fictional liberties with the location and condition. If you want to know more about it, check out *White Otter Castle : the legacy of Jimmy McOuat* by Elinor Barr, Thunder Bay, Ont. : Singing Shield Productions, 1984. There is also *The Castle of White Otter Lake* [dvd] / directed by Peter Elliott. Ontario : Railway Town Productions, [2010]. A number of tours are available online as well as information on several ways to reach the castle on your own.

Connect with the Author

Bonnie Ferrante is on Facebook (Bonnie Ferrante - Author), Twitter, Linkedin, and has her own website at BonnieFerrante.ca. She is also on Goodreads and has an Author Page on Amazon. If you enjoyed this book, a positive review would be greatly appreciated.